KT-398-903

GO AHEAD, SECRET SEVEN

Have you got them all?

GO AHEAD, SECRET SEVEN

ENID BLYTON

Illustrated by George Brook

Hodder
Children's
Books

a division of Hachette Children's Books

Copyright © Chorion Rights Ltd
Enid Blyton's signature mark and the Secret Seven are Trade Marks
of Chorion Rights Ltd
All rights reserved.

This edition first published in 2009
by Hodder Children's Books

The right of Enid Blyton to be identified as the Author of
the Work has been asserted by her in accordance with the
Copyright, Designs and Patent Act 1988.

1

All rights reserved. Apart from any use permitted under UK copyright
law, this publication may only be reproduced, stored or transmitted,
in any form, or by any means with prior permission in writing from
the publishers or in the case of reprographic production in accordance
with the terms of licences issued by the Copyright Licensing Agency
and may not be otherwise circulated in any form of binding or cover
other than that in which it is published and without a similar
condition being imposed on the subsequent purchaser.

All characters in this publication are fictitious and any
resemblance to real persons, living or dead, is purely coincidental.

A Catalogue record for this book is available from the British Library

ISBN-13: 978 0 340 68095 7

Typeset in Times by Avon DataSet Ltd,
Bidford-on-Avon, Warwickshire

Printed and bound in Great Britain by
CPI Group (UK) Ltd, Croydon, CR0 4YY

The paper and board used in this paperback by Hodder Children's Books
are natural reyclable products made from wood grown in sustainable forests.
The manufacturing processes conform to the environmental regulations
of the country of origin.

Hodder Children's Books
a division of Hachette Children's Books
338 Euston Road, London NW1 3BH
An Hachette UK Company
www.hachette.co.uk

Contents

CHAPTER ONE

Susie is most annoying

PETER WAS going home from school one afternoon, swinging his satchel, when someone came running behind him and bumped into him.

He dropped his bag and almost fell over. He looked round crossly, expecting it to be George or Colin. But it wasn't. It was Susie with her cheeky face, standing by the kerb grinning at him.

'Sorry!' she said. 'You were in my way. How's the Secret Seven Society going?'

'You just look where you're going, Susie,' said Peter, picking up his bag. 'As for the Secret Seven, it's no business of *yours*. You're always trying to interfere!'

1

'Jack says there haven't been any Secret Seven meetings for ages,' said Susie, walking beside Peter, much to his annoyance. Susie was the most aggravating girl he knew.

Jack was Susie's brother, and a member of the Secret Seven. Peter was quite sure he hadn't said anything about the meetings. But Susie was right. They hadn't had any meetings for a long time. The Easter term had been rather exciting so far, and Peter hadn't thought a great deal about his secret society.

'Well, we're having a Secret Seven meeting very soon,' he said to Susie, making up his mind suddenly that they would. 'But you're not coming! And if you try any silly snooping, you'll be sorry. You don't belong to our Society, and you never will.'

'I know your last password,' said Susie, skipping over the cracks in the paving-stones. 'Aha!'

'You don't,' said Peter, racking his brains to remember what it was. Goodness – it wouldn't do for *him* to forget it!

'I do. It's Jack Sprat!' said Susie, and Peter scowled at her. She was right. Jack Sprat was the last password they had chosen – a secret password – and here was Susie shouting it out in the road. She saw his angry face and laughed.

'I'm right, aren't I? Yours is a silly society. I know your password, and so do all the girls in my class. I told them. So the next time you have a meeting we'll all be along, shout out the password, and you'll have to let us in.'

'Who told you the password?' demanded Peter. 'I know Jack wouldn't.'

'Oh no. Jack's a most annoying brother. He never tells me anything,' said Susie. 'But when I went to borrow a hanky from his drawer, I found a piece of paper there, hidden under a pile of hankies. And on it was scribbled: "Remember the password – Jack Sprat".'

'You're always snooping about, Susie!' said Peter, angrily. 'I never knew such a girl. Why can't you leave us alone, and not keep trying to find out our passwords and what we're doing?'

'Well, why don't you let me belong?' demanded Susie. 'You let Janet belong, and Pam and Barbara.'

'Don't be silly. It's the Secret *Seven*. We can't have any more members, or we'd be eight,' said Peter. 'Anyway, we don't want you, Susie.'

'You're mean,' said Susie. 'Well, I'll tell Jack you're having another meeting soon. When shall I say it is?'

'Don't you go telling Jack anything!' said Peter, really exasperated with this annoying sister of Jack's. '*I* send out notices of meetings, not you. And you needn't bother to remember the password. I shall choose another one immediately, and let the members know.'

'Oh, well, Jack is sure to write it down to remember it again,' said Susie, skipping off. 'And I shall be sure to find it. Goodbye, and give my love to Jack Sprat.'

Peter glared at Susie's back. What an awful girl! He was glad that his own sister, Janet, wasn't like Susie. He walked home with a solemn face.

Certainly a meeting must be called soon.

There hadn't been one for ages. It would never do to let the Secret Seven come to an end just because there weren't any meetings, or anything special happening.

But you can't solve mysteries and things unless there are some to solve, thought Peter. We'll have to think up something else to do, till one comes along. Sometimes it seems as if nothing happens for ages and ages. I'll have to change the password, too. Fancy Jack being such an idiot as to write down the password in case he forgot it. He might have known that Susie would find it.

He went home, thinking hard. Janet, his sister, was already there, and Scamper, the golden spaniel, came rushing out to greet him, barking with joy.

'Hallo, Scamper! Been a good dog today?' said Peter, fondling the long, silky ears. 'Eaten all your dinner? Been sniffing for rabbits? Barked at the dustman? You have? Ah, you're a *very* good dog, then!'

'Woof!' said Scamper, and raced round the room like a mad dog.

Janet laughed. 'He knew you were coming

long before you came in at the door,' she said. 'He sat with his head on one side, listening for about three minutes before you came in. He must have known when you turned the corner up the lane.'

'Janet,' said Peter, putting down his satchel of books. 'We've got to call a Secret Seven meeting as soon as possible.'

'Oh, good! But why? Has anything happened?' said Janet, thrilled. She was disappointed when Peter shook his head.

'No – except that I met that awful sister of Jack's – Susie. And she's found out the password, and she was jeering at us because we haven't had a meeting for ages. So we simply must have one, and we must choose a new password, too! Get out your notepaper, and we'll arrange a meeting as soon as we can.'

CHAPTER TWO

Secret Seven meeting

THE SECRET Seven meeting was called for the very next day, immediately after school. Peter's mother was told, and she suggested that all the members should come to tea first, and have the meeting afterwards.

'I'll wash up every single thing after the meeting,' said Janet. 'Hurrah! Another Secret Seven meeting. How pleased everyone will be!'

The notes were sent out, and the Secret Seven were thrilled. Jack went scrabbling in his drawer to find the bit of paper on which he had written the password. He found it, but he was *most* surprised when he read it. This is what he read:

'Remember the password – Jack Sprat. No, Jack Horner. No, Jack the Giant-Killer. No – it's Jack and Jill!'

Jack stared at the bit of scribbled paper, frowning. Whatever had made him write all that? He must have been mad. And which was the password? He was sure it was Jack Sprat.

He looked closely at the paper. 'Bother Susie! She's written half of it! She's been snooping in my drawer and found the paper, and read the password! Just wait till I see her!'

But fortunately for Susie she was out to tea. Jack hunted for his badge, and at last found it. He had been afraid that Susie might have discovered that too. Really, she was the most annoying sister in the world!

The tea-party was fixed for half-past four, after school. Janet and Peter had carried everything down, and the shed looked very warm and cosy. They had a small oil stove in one corner for warmth, six candles stuck here and there, and a box for a table. Janet had put a cloth on it.

Two enormous jugs of hot cocoa stood there, with seven mugs round it. Ranged on a shelf behind were seven plates of food.

'Honey sandwiches, sardine sandwiches – and I hope you won't go for those too much, Peter, you're a pig over sardines,' said Janet. 'Buns buttered and jammed, all in halves. New doughnuts. A chocolate cake baked today. A smashing jam-sponge sandwich, already cut into seven by Mummy. Doesn't it look lovely? Oh – and a plate of mixed biscuits.'

'Woof!' said Scamper at once, and his tail thumped hard on the ground.

'*Your* dish of goodies is on the floor, but you're not to begin your tea till we do,' said Janet. Scamper looked at his own plate and sniffed longingly.

He saw two sardine sandwiches, made of the tails and little bones; one bun cut in half, with just a scraping of butter, but no jam, because Scamper liked his without; and a very large dog-biscuit smeared with potted meat. What a tea for a hungry dog!

'Here they come,' said Janet, as they heard footsteps coming down the path to the shed.

She peered out of the window. 'It's Pam and Barbara.'

Rap-rap!

'Password!' called out Peter.

'Jack Sprat,' came the answer, and Peter opened the door at once. No sooner was it shut than more footsteps were heard, and another knock.

'Password?'

'Er – I'm most awfully sorry, Peter, but it's such ages since we had a meeting that I've forgotten it,' said a voice, sounding rather upset. Janet glanced at Peter. Was he going to be cross, and perhaps refuse to let in poor Colin?

No. Peter didn't look at all cross. He opened the door, and Colin came in, looking most relieved.

'Hello!' he said, staring in delight at the tea.

'I'm sorry about the password, but, honestly, it's ages since we used it.'

'It's all right,' said Peter. 'It was my fault for not calling a meeting before. Anyway, that awful sister of Jack's knows it, so we've got to choose a new one.'

Rap-rap-rap-RAP!

'Password!' called Peter.

'Jack Sprat!' said two voices, and in came George and Jack, complete with Secret Seven badges. The door shut. The candles gave a wavering light in the rather dark shed, and everything looked cosy, and rather mysterious. Just the kind of thing the Secret Seven liked!

'What's the meeting about?' said Jack, sitting on an upturned flower-pot. 'Anything special?'

'No,' said Peter. 'Nothing's turned up, worse luck – but we can't let our Society fizzle out because we wait and wait for something to happen. We'll talk about that later. Pour out the cocoa, Janet, and remember that we all like heaps of sugar.'

'Woof! woof!' said Scamper, approvingly, and got a lump of sugar from Janet at once. She poured out the cocoa, and Peter handed round the sandwiches. Soon everyone was tucking in, and Scamper gulped down his sandwiches and his bun in no time, and then settled down happily to crunch his potted-meat biscuit.

In ten minutes' time every plate was empty. Not even a biscuit was left. Jack sat back with a sigh. 'That was a scrumptious tea,' he said. 'Any more cocoa left?'

'Half a mug each,' said Janet. 'Pass yours up.'

'While we're having our last drink, we'll begin the meeting,' said Peter. 'It's not a very *important* meeting, but we've got quite a bit to discuss and to plan. If this Secret Seven hasn't any particular job to work on, it's got to find other things to do. Do you agree, members?'

'We do,' said everyone, pleased.

'Right,' said Peter. 'Well, I'll begin. Stop thumping your tail on the floor, Scamper, and you listen too!'

CHAPTER THREE

A new password – and a few ideas

EVERYONE SAT quiet. Scamper stopped his tail-thumping and sat still too, his head on one side. He was very, very proud to be at all the meetings, even though he wasn't a proper member.

'First of all,' said Peter, 'we must choose a new password, partly because Susie knows it!'

Jack was startled. How did Peter know that Susie knew it? 'Yes, she does know it,' he said, and fished the piece of paper out of his pocket, on which he had written the old password, and on which Susie had scribbled her nonsense.

'Look there, she found this bit of paper, with our password on it. I wrote it down so that I wouldn't forget it, and I hid it, and she found it and scribbled on it! But how did you *know* she knew it, Peter?'

'She told me,' said Peter. 'She seemed to think our Society was about to come to an end, or something, and she was so annoying that it made me decide to call a meeting at once. Jack, for goodness' sake don't leave our passwords about again!'

'All right. I won't,' said Jack, looking rather red in the face. 'But you don't know what it is to have a sister like Susie. I wouldn't be surprised if she isn't trying to peep in at the window this very minute.'

Everyone at once looked up at the little window, Scamper too. Peter shook his head.

'No, nobody's about. Scamper would bark if

17

he heard the slightest sound. Well, what about a new password? Anyone got a good idea?'

'Snooper!' said Colin, thinking of Susie. 'That would be a good one.'

'Yes, we'd all remember that because of Susie,' said Janet.

'We'll have to remember the password is *Snooper*, not *Susie*,' said Pam, with a giggle. 'I'm sure I shall say "Susie" if anyone asks me the password next week!'

Jack often felt cross with his sister, but he didn't very much like the idea of the password being chosen because of Susie's snoopy behaviour. After all, she *was* his sister, and although she was very annoying at times, he was fond of her. He shook his head.

'No. I don't want that password, if you don't mind. I've got a better one. One that nobody would ever think of. What about "Beware!"? It sounds sort of *suitable* for us.'

'Yes, it does,' agreed Peter, and the others nodded their heads. They began to say the password to one another, in hollow, mysterious voices, and Scamper looked rather startled.

'Beware!' Janet said to Barbara, solemnly.

'Be-warrrrrrr!' hissed Colin to Jack.

'BEWARE!' said Peter to Scamper, who got up at once and sniffed in every corner of the shed, as if he had to discover what it was that everyone was warning him about. Beware! Well, he would beware all right, but what of?

'Look at Scamper. He's puzzled to bits,' said Pam, with a laugh. 'It's all right, Scamper. It's just our new password. Well, I don't think *any* of us will forget it. It's a very good one. Beware! It makes me feel quite creepy.'

19

'The next thing to discuss is what the Secret Seven are to do,' said Peter. 'I suppose nobody has heard of anything peculiar or mysterious or extraordinary that we could look into?'

Nobody said a word. They just looked at one another hopefully, and then shook their heads.

'Well, as there's nothing peculiar to make plans about, we'll have to decide something to *do*,' said Peter. 'I mean, it's been such a long time since we held a meeting, and societies just fizzle out if they're not kept going somehow. We must *do* something to keep up our interest or when something *does* come along, we'll miss it.'

'Yes, but what do you mean, *do* something?' asked Colin. 'We can't *make* things happen.'

'No. I know that,' said Peter. 'But we can put in a bit of practice. We can set ourselves one or two things to do.'

'What, for instance?' said George.

'Well, we could practise shadowing people,' said Peter. 'And we might perhaps have a shot at disguising ourselves, just to see if we could get away with it.'

'Disguising ourselves? But how could we?'

said Pam. 'We're only children. We can't wear false beards, or ragged clothes, or pretend to walk with limps or anything. We'd be spotted at once.'

'Well, perhaps that's not such a good idea,' admitted Peter. 'We'll leave that for the minute. But we could practise spotting somebody, and then writing down a very clear description of him, so as to get practice at that kind of thing. It's always useful to be able to describe a thief in great detail, for instance.'

'But how do we know who's a thief?' said Jack.

'We don't,' said Peter, beginning to be impatient. 'We just go, say, to the railway station, and sit down on a seat. We watch the people standing there waiting for a train. We pick on somebody, it doesn't matter who. We look at them carefully, and memorise everything about them. Then, when they've gone, we write down what we've remembered. It would be very, very good practice for observing people.'

'It sounds rather dull to me,' said George. 'I'd much sooner do some shadowing or something. Anyway, I'm not much good at describing anything. I'm always bottom in composition at school. I just can't think of a thing to say.'

'All right, you can do the shadowing,' said Peter. 'Perhaps the girls would be better at spotting people and describing them.'

'Woof!' said Scamper, suddenly. 'Woof!'

'Somebody's about,' said Peter. 'Quick, open the door and let Scamper out. If it's Susie we'll give her the fright of her life!'

CHAPTER FOUR

What fun to belong to a Secret Society!

IT WASN'T Susie. It was Peter's mother coming to say that it was getting late, and did they know what the time was? She was very surprised to meet Scamper flying out of the door in the greatest excitement, barking for all he was worth. He was quite disappointed that it was only Peter's mother!

'Oh, Mother, it *can't* be half-past six yet,' groaned Peter. 'We haven't nearly finished the meeting. Yes, I know we haven't done our homework, but we haven't much tonight. Can't we have another ten minutes?'

'Yes. Ten minutes, then,' said his mother, and went away. The door was shut again, and the Secret Seven began to talk hurriedly.

'George, you can do a spot of shadowing, and so can Colin,' said Peter. 'You girls can do the observation idea, go to the station or the bus-stop, or anywhere. Jack, you can I will do a bit of spying. We'll find a good spying-place, sit there, and watch what goes on without being seen. It will be good practice for when we *really* have to do it!'

'How do we do the shadowing?' asked George. 'We'd be seen following anybody in broad daylight.'

'Well, do it when it's dark, then,' said Peter. 'But don't go shadowing anyone together, you and Colin, or you'll be spotted at once. That would be silly. Go separately, choose someone you see, and follow them to their home without being seen. If you can do that, you'll be very smart!'

'I'd rather tackle a *real* mystery or problem than mess about practising,' said George, in a grumbling voice.

'I'm the head of this society, and you have to obey orders,' said Peter in rather a haughty voice. 'I've got to keep the Secret Seven going, haven't I? Well, I'm doing my best.'

'Anyway, you never know when we *might* come across something when we're putting in a bit of practice in these things,' said Jack, cheerfully. 'Things pop up most unexpectedly.'

'We'll practise our observation stunt on Saturday morning,' said Janet. 'I'll go to the railway station. I always like that, it's nice and busy and noisy.'

'I'll go to the bus-stop,' said Pam. 'You come with me, Barbara.'

'Right,' said Peter, pleased. 'Now we've all got secret jobs to do, and they'll keep us going till something turns up. Jack, I'll let you know when I've thought of a good place for us to hide and keep a watch on any goings-on nearby.'

Everyone got up, sorry that the meeting had come to an end. Pam and Barbara offered to help Janet wash up, and all the boys carried in the dirty plates and mugs for the girls.

'Now for homework,' said Peter, with a groan. 'I wish I'd listened better in class this morning. I haven't the faintest idea how to do those sums we've been set.'

Pam, Jack and George said good night, and thanked Peter's mother for the 'delicious' tea. The others washed up together, chattering at the

tops of their voices. They didn't say a word of
what had happened at the meeting, of course.
Nobody was ever supposed to tell anything that
had passed at one of the Secret Seven
gatherings.

But all the members thought about it a lot. It
was fun to belong to a secret society. It was
something you could hug to yourself and think
about before you went to sleep at night. Janet
looked at her Secret Seven badge that evening
when she took it off her dress.

'S.S.,' she said. 'It should really be *five* Ss. S.S.S.S.S. For Super, Smashing, Secret, Seven, Society! I must remember to tell Peter that. I'll go to the station on Saturday morning, and watch for someone to describe perfectly. I won't miss a thing, not even the colour of his tie! I'll show the others how good I am at noticing every single thing about somebody I see just for a minute.'

Peter was thinking about what he and Jack could do, too, as he lay in bed that night. A spyhole? Now, where would an *interesting* one be? In the middle of the bush beside the main road? Yes, that would be a good place. They could take note-books and note down the cars that went by. They could put down anything they thought was interesting or suspicious. It would be fun!

Each member was planning carefully what he or she was to do. George was perhaps making the most careful plans of all. He was to go and shadow somebody. Well, he would do it really properly! He would first of all hide somewhere, and watch for somebody to come by. Then he would slip out and follow them, oh, so carefully and quietly! He would put on his rubber shoes.

'And I'll creep behind in the shadows, just like a policeman following a thief or a spy!' he thought. 'I'll be like a shadow myself. Nobody will know I'm there. I'll choose a man with a bag, to make it more real. I'll pretend he's got stolen maps in it, or jewels or something. Gosh, I'm going to enjoy this!'

All the Seven fell asleep at last. What fun it was to belong to a secret society!

CHAPTER FIVE

A little shadowing

'PETER, WHEN is the next meeting, do you suppose?' asked Janet, on Saturday morning. 'I'm going to the station now, to do my practice for the Secret Seven, you know, watching somebody and describing them, and I'd like to know when I can give my work in to the Society. I'm going to do it really well.'

'Well, I'll call the meeting for one evening next week,' said Peter. 'That will be time enough. I'm going off now to find a good spyhole with Jack. Have I got my notebook and pencil? Yes, I have. Well, good luck at the station, Janet, and don't choose just one person. That would be too easy. Choose three at least.'

'I thought I'd choose somebody we all know, too, if I can,' said Janet. 'Then you'll see if you can recognise them when I read out my notes.'

'Good idea,' said Peter. 'Well, I'm off to call for Jack.'

He set off, and Janet went in the opposite direction, to the station. She passed Barbara and Pam on the way. They were sitting on the bus-stop seat, looking rather giggly, with notebooks in their hands.

'Have you begun yet?' asked Janet, in a low voice.

'No. No bus has stopped here yet,' said Pam. 'We're each going to choose one passenger getting out, and wait till the bus has gone off again. Then we're going to put down

exactly what we remember about the two passengers.'

Colin and George were not thinking about their Secret Seven jobs just then. Both had decided to do them at night. Shadowing would be so much easier then. They were not going together, of course. Peter had forbidden that.

But when the evening came, only George set out. Colin had sneezed three times, and his mother had heard him. As she knew he caught colds very easily, she wouldn't let him go out after tea!

'But, Mother, I *must*,' said Colin, desperately. 'It's Secret Seven work. I've *got* to do it.'

'Can't it be done another night?' said his mother. 'Surely it isn't absolutely necessary to do it tonight.'

Colin hesitated. 'Well, yes, I suppose it *could* be done another night,' he said truthfully. 'All right, Mother, I won't go tonight. But you *will* let me go another night, won't you?'

So only George went out shadowing that night. He had put on rubber shoes so that he made no sound when walking or running. He had put on a dark overcoat, so that he wouldn't be seen in the shadows. He had even blacked his face. He looked most peculiar!

He stared at himself in the mirror and grinned, so that his teeth suddenly showed startlingly white in his black face. 'I'd better slip out of the garden door,' he decided. 'If Mother catches sight of me she'll have a fit! I do look strange!'

He decided to take a rubber truncheon that he had had for Christmas, to make it seem more real. Now I can really pretend I'm a policeman! he thought, swinging the rubber truncheon from his wrist. It looked exactly like a real one, but was only made of thin brown rubber!

He crept downstairs and out of the garden door. His rubber shoes made no sound. He went down the path to the back gate and came out quietly into the dark street. The street lamps were lit. He would have to keep out of their radiance.

He went along cautiously, swinging the rubber truncheon. Now then, you thieves! Now then, you spies! Look out, here comes P.C. Rubber-Soles, hard on your trail!

Who was he to shadow? Nobody seemed to come along at all. Wait a minute, was this the bus coming? Yes, it was. Good! It would set some passengers down, and he could trail one of them to his home, wherever it was.

The bus stopped up the street, and George saw some black shadows moving as people stepped down from it. Somebody was walking towards him now, having got off the bus. He would shadow him! George pressed himself back into the hedge, and waited, scarcely daring to breathe.

The man came along. He was a tall, stooping fellow, wearing a hat, and carrying a bag. Good! Suppose there were stolen jewels in that bag! George would trail him right to his home, and he would then know where this supposed robber lived!

It seemed very real somehow, not pretence. The night was dark, the man came along without guessing that a boy was pressing himself into the shadows of a bush, and George suddenly found his heart beginning to thump. The man passed.

Now to follow him without being seen. If he spotted George, then George had failed. But George was certain he could shadow the man right back to his house without once being seen.

He came out from the bush and began to follow the man, keeping well into the darkness of the trees that lined the road. Down the road to the corner. Round the corner. Be careful now, *creep* round the corner, in case the man knows he is being followed!

George crept round cautiously, his rubber truncheon in his hand, pretending to himself that there might be great danger from a fierce thief!

He heaved a sigh of relief. There was the man, halfway down the road. George trotted on after him. Look behind you, George, as well as in front. Quick, George, look behind you!

CHAPTER SIX

A shock for poor George

BUT GEORGE didn't look behind him. He only looked in front, and followed the man steadily. Once, when he stopped to tie his shoelace, George darted into a nearby gate, afraid that the man might turn and see him.

He crept out after half a minute, and saw the

man walking on again, swinging his bag. After him went George, deciding to get a little nearer, so that he could see exactly where the man lived when he went into his house.

So he crept quite near, feeling very bold and successful. And then suddenly something happened.

George heard sudden footsteps behind him, and then a heavy hand fell on his shoulder and a sharp voice spoke loudly.

'And what do you think *you* are doing, creeping along in the dark after that gentleman in front? What's this you've got on your wrist? A truncheon! Don't tell me you meant to use it, you wicked little scoundrel!'

George was so astounded that he couldn't say a word. He stared up at the man, who dragged him to a nearby lamp-post.

'What have you done to your face?' said the man.

He was a young fellow, strong and determined-looking, and he gave George a sudden shake.

'Have you lost your tongue?' He dabbed at George's face, and whistled. 'You've blacked it. What for? Are you one of the wretched little

37

hooligans who think they can hit innocent people, rob them and run away?' demanded the young man, and shook George roughly again.

George found his tongue. 'Let me go!' he said, indignantly. 'Of course I'm not a hooligan! I'm only shadowing somebody for, well, just for practice!'

'I don't believe a word of it,' said the man. 'I've followed you right from the bus, you little wretch! I watched you hiding here and there,

creeping round the corners, following that old fellow with the bag. Come along with me. I'll take you to the police-station. You can tell your tale there!'

George was really frightened now. He tried to wriggle away, but the man held him too tightly.

'Please don't take me to the police-station,' begged George. 'My mother would be so upset. Take me home. I'll tell you my name and address, and come with you. You'll see I'm a good boy, not a hooligan. I wouldn't DREAM of following anyone to rob them.'

'All right. I'll take you to your home,' said the young man, grimly. 'And I'll have a word with your father, young man. What you want is a good talking to!'

And poor George had to trot beside him all the way home, held so tightly by his collar that he could hardly breathe.

He didn't have at all a pleasant time at home. The young man made his harmless adventure seem very, very serious. His mother was shocked. His father was angry.

'Well, I didn't mean any harm,' said poor

George, rather sulky now. 'It was only the orders I had from Peter, who is the head of the Secret Seven, our society. We were just practising several things, in case some mystery or other turned up. That's all. I had to shadow someone, and I did. But there wasn't any *harm* in it!'

'I see,' said his father. 'Well, that's the end of the Secret Society for you, George. If I'm going to have you hauled home by a member of the public, accusing you of following some

harmless old fellow, and carrying a truncheon, and with your face blacked, well, all I can say is that the Secret Society is leading you into bad ways.'

'I agree,' said his mother. 'He mustn't belong any more.'

George looked at his parents in the utmost dismay. 'But, Dad! Mother! You don't understand. I couldn't *possibly* not belong to the Secret Seven. They wouldn't let me go. I *must* belong!'

'That's enough, George,' said his father, curtly. 'You know I won't be argued with. Go and wash that black off your face, and tell this Secret Society of yours tomorrow that you no longer belong. Do you hear me?'

'Yes, Dad,' said George, shocked and miserable. He said good night in a low voice, gave the young man a fearful scowl, and went out of the room. He debated whether to slam the door or not, but decided not to. His father did not look kindly on any show of temper.

Poor George! He washed his black face, undressed, and got into bed. What a dreadful thing not to belong to the Secret Seven any more! What would they do without him? They would only be Six. Would they call themselves the Secret Six? That would still be S.S.

Or, dreadful thought, would they get someone else instead of him? George felt as if he really could *not* bear that. He buried his face in his pillow and gritted his teeth. It was too bad! He had only done what Peter had told him, and he had done it very well too, and that horrid young man had thought he was up to mischief and had hauled him home.

Tomorrow he must go and tell Peter and Janet. They would have to call a meeting on Monday night and decide what to do without him. He would be there for the last time. He would never, never attend one of those exciting secret meetings after that.

'I shall howl if I go on thinking like this,' said George fiercely, and hit his pillow hard, pretending it was the young man who had caught him. 'Take that! And that!'

He felt better then, but it was a long time before he fell asleep. Poor George!

CHAPTER SEVEN

George resigns –
and a new member is elected

ON MONDAY evening, immediately after school, a meeting of the Secret Seven was called. All the Seven knew why. It was about George.

George had gone to see Peter on Sunday

morning, and had told him what had happened. Peter was shocked.

'We must call a meeting as soon as possible,' he said, 'to see what we can do about it. Poor George! This is awful!'

So a very solemn, serious meeting was held down in the little shed that had the S.S. sign on its door. George gave the password in rather a trembling voice as he went in, and wore his badge for the last time.

'Beware!' he said, and at the password the door was opened. Everyone was there, Scamper as well.

'Hello, George,' said Janet, feeling very miserable to see George's woebegone face. 'Bad luck!'

'I expect Peter's told you what happened,' said George, sitting down on a box. 'It was just, well, what Janet said just now, bad luck!'

George took off his badge and handed it to Peter, who pinned it carefully to his jersey, beside his own badge.

'I now resign from the Secret Seven,' said George, in rather a shaky voice. 'Thank you for letting me belong. I'm very, very sorry to go, but my father says I must.'

'It's horrid of him!' said Pam fiercely, very sorry for George.

But George was not going to have anything said against his father, much as he resented being forced to leave the Secret Seven.

'He's not horrid,' he said, loyally. 'It was that young man's fault. He caused all the trouble, making such a fuss about me. He *knew* I wasn't doing any harm. He's the mean, horrid one, not my father.'

'Who was he? Do you know?' asked Jack.

'No idea,' said George. 'I'd never seen him before. When Dad asked him for his address, he said that he lived at that little hotel called "Starling's". He didn't give his name.'

'I've a good mind to go and find out who he is and tell him what I think of him!' said Jack, scowling.

'Yes. That's a good idea,' said Peter. 'Colin, Jack and I will all go. It's the least we can do for old George. We'll tell that young man what we think of him!'

'He'll just haul you home too, and get *you*

into trouble!' said George, feeling rather comforted by all the interest on his behalf. 'I must say I couldn't understand why he was so interfering. Even when I told him who I was and where I lived, he was just as mean.'

'Starling's Hotel,' said Peter, and wrote it down firmly in his note-book. 'We'll go and ask for him and tell him he's done a really mean thing.'

'I'll come, too,' said Pam, bravely; but Peter said no, the three of them could manage by themselves.

'What are you going to do about the Secret Seven now?' asked George after a pause. 'I mean, you're only six, now I'm out of it. Will you be the Secret Six?'

'No,' said Peter. 'We began as the Secret Seven, and we'll have to go on as the Secret Seven. You can't suddenly change a society as important as ours.'

'I see,' said George. 'Well, you'll have to get a seventh, then. I shall hate that. Who will you have? Lennie, or Richard?'

'No,' said Peter, firmly, and everyone looked at him to see who was in his mind.

'Hadn't we better all put up somebody's name, and then we'll vote?' asked Colin. 'That's if we've got to have someone else. I shan't much like anyone in George's place.'

'You will ALL like the one that I'm thinking of, I promise you,' said Peter, and his eyes twinkled at them. 'Nobody will say no, I promise you!'

'Who is it?' said poor George, wondering

who this wonderful person was that everyone would welcome.

'Yes, who is it?' said Janet, puzzled.

'He's with us tonight,' said Peter. 'But he will only be a temporary member, not a member for good, just a temporary member till we get George back again. Because I'm determined to go and find that young man and make him go and ask George's parents to let him belong to the Secret Seven again. I bet he didn't know how important it is to George to belong.'

'But who's the temporary member?' said George, puzzled. He looked all round. 'There's nobody here but us.'

'It's Scamper!' said Peter, and Scamper leapt up at his name, and wagged his tail vigorously. 'Scamper, will you please be a proper member of the Secret Seven till we get George back?'

'Woof, *woof*, woof!' said Scamper, joyously, as if he understood completely. Everyone began to laugh, even George.

'Oh, Peter!' he said. 'Scamper's the only person I don't mind taking my place! He's always *really* belonged to the Secret Seven, hasn't he? Oh, I do hope I come back. Still, I don't feel so bad now that Scamper's the seventh member. I just felt I couldn't bear to know that Lennie or Richard belonged instead of me.'

Everybody felt more cheerful. Scamper ran round and licked all the knees and hands he could see.

'Just as if he's saying "Thank you, thank you for this great honour,"' said Jack. 'Good old Scamper! Peter, pin the badge to his collar. Scamper, please remember the password. Let me say it in your ear, BEWARE!'

The meeting broke up. George said goodbye rather solemnly. Scamper took the members proudly to the gate, and then turned back. Wait till he showed the other dogs his magnificent badge!

CHAPTER EIGHT

A few reports

ANOTHER SECRET Seven meeting was held the next night, to hear the result of the various 'observations' and 'watchings'. All the seven were there, but the seventh this time was Scamper, not George. It seemed strange without him.

It was quite a business-like meeting. Janet spoke first. She took out her notebook and read from it.

'I was at the railway station,' she said, 'and I picked out three people to observe as they passed. They came off the 10.13 train from Pilberry.

'First, an old woman with a round face, a big nose with a wart at one side, and grey curly hair. She wore a green coat with a belt, a hat with lots of red cherries round it and . . .'

'Mrs Lawson!' yelled everyone at once, and Janet looked pleased.

'Yes,' she said. 'Quite right. I chose her just to see if I could describe her well enough for you to recognise. Here's the second person, not very exciting. A young woman in a nurse's uniform, golden hair, doll-like face, small feet and a quick walk.'

'Well, it's quite a good *short* description,' said Peter. 'I feel as if I might know her if I saw her. I think you're good at this, Janet.'

Janet went red with pleasure. She loved Peter to praise her. 'Here's my last,' she said. 'I chose him because he really was a bit peculiar. Listen.

'A very stoopy man, who walked a bit lame, had an old soft hat pulled well down over his face, a long overcoat with the shoulders very square, small feet for his size, a funny hand . . .'

'What do you mean, a funny hand?' asked Peter.

'Well, I don't quite know what was the matter with it,' said Janet. 'It looked as if two fingers were missing, and it was sort of deformed and crooked. That's all.'

'Colour of his hair, his tie or scarf, and how did he walk – quick, slow or medium?' asked Peter.

'His hat was too low, I couldn't see his hair, and he had no tie or scarf,' said Janet. 'And he limped a bit. There! Do you think you would recognise *him* if you saw him?'

'Oh yes!' said everyone. 'Well done, Janet.'

'Now you, Barbara and Pam,' said Peter. But their notes proved to be rather silly.

'They sound as if you'd had one of your stupid giggling fits,' said Peter, reprovingly. 'Don't read any more. They wouldn't be a *bit* of use if we were *really* trying to find out something. Very poor, both of you. Now you, Colin. Did you do any shadowing?'

'No,' said Colin. 'I began a cold on Saturday night, so my mother wouldn't let me. I'm doing it tonight, after this meeting. I'm sorry, but it wasn't my fault.'

'Right,' said Peter. 'Well, that only leaves me and Jack. We found a good spyhole in a thick clump of leafy twigs springing out round the trunk of a great elm-tree. They hid us beautifully. We sat there, peeping through the leaves, and at first we saw nothing.'

'Not many people walk along that road,' explained Jack. 'It's Fairmile Road, and you know how long it is. Most people take a bus. We didn't see anyone for ages.'

'In fact, we haven't much to report,' said Peter. 'The only possible thing of interest we saw was a car that came by, and stopped just near us.'

'But why was that interesting?' asked Pam.

'Well, it *wasn't* very interesting, actually,' said Peter. 'All that happened was that a man got out with a dog, a magnificent grey poodle, fluffy in patches and bare in patches, you know how poodles look! The dog was terribly frightened, I thought. But you could see it was only car-sick and it soon recovered, and began to sniff round quite naturally.'

'It didn't like going back into the car, though,' said Jack. 'It whined like anything and pulled away from the man as hard as it could. He was pretty rough with it, I thought.'

'I suppose the poor thing knew it would be car-sick again,' said Janet. 'Do you remember our next-door neighbour's dog, Peter? Every time it went out in the car, it cried and cried because it felt so ill.'

'Well, your report doesn't seem *very* interesting,' said Barbara, rather glad to repay Peter for his candid remarks about her report and Pam's. 'Did you take the car's number? I bet you didn't.'

'There wasn't much point in taking it,' said Peter. 'But as it happens, we did. Here it is – PSD 188.'

'PSD – pretty sick dog!' said Colin. 'That's easy enough to remember!'

There was a laugh, and then a pause. Peter shut his notebook.

'Well, that's all,' he said. 'I don't really feel we've done very much that is useful. Janet's reports are the best. They show how good she would be if she had to describe someone seen for only half a minute. The police are always asking for descriptions of persons seen by the public, and hardly anyone ever seems to be able to remember much about any stranger they saw.'

'But Janet would be able to tell them everything,' said Pam, rather jealously.

'The only big thing that has come out of this practice idea is George having to leave the Secret Seven,' said Colin, gloomily. 'Well, is it worth while my doing my bit of shadowing tonight, Peter? I mean, we don't seem to have done anything much, and I don't want to get caught like George.'

'George should have looked behind him as well as in front,' said Peter. 'You won't make that mistake. I think you should do your bit, Colin. I've a good mind to make Pam and Barbara do their bits again too!'

But the girls looked so crossly at him that he decided to say no more!

Colin got up. 'Well, I'm going on my job,' he said. 'What are you all going to do?'

'Let's go indoors and play a game,' suggested Janet. 'There are five of us left – sorry, Scamper, six – I forgot you! We've got an hour before it's supper-time. Come along in, Pam, Barbara and Jack.'

So they all five went in, and were soon playing a peaceful game of cards. But it wasn't peaceful for long! Who was that rapping at the window?

Tap-tap-tap! Tap-tap-tap!

'Quick! Open the window. I've something to tell you all!'

CHAPTER NINE

Colin's strange tale

'OPEN THE window!' said Janet putting down her cards. 'It's Colin! What's happened?'

Peter opened the window, and Colin climbed in. He was panting. 'Thanks,' he said. 'I didn't like to come to the front door or the back, in case your mother saw me and asked me what

was up. So I tapped at the window. I saw you inside, playing cards.'

'What's happened?' said Peter. 'You're dirty, and your hand's bleeding.'

'Oh, that's nothing,' said Colin. 'Listen! You know I left you to go and find somebody to shadow, don't you?'

'Yes,' said everyone.

'Well, I didn't see anyone at first,' said Colin, 'and it began to rain and I was pretty fed up. So I chose to shadow the very first person I saw.'

'Who was that?' said Jack.

'A young man with a dog,' said Colin. 'I thought he must be taking it out for an evening walk. It didn't seem to like the walk very much. It kept whining and pulling away from the man, and I thought it might smell me, following quietly along some way behind, but it didn't seem to. I couldn't see what the dog was like at first, because it's a dark evening and raining. Then, when the man and the dog walked beneath a street lamp, I saw it.'

'What was it?' asked Janet.

'It was a bull-terrier,' said Colin. 'A beauty.

A real beauty. My mother's friend breeds them, so I know a good one when I see it. Well, I shadowed the man and the dog, and it was really pretty easy, because the man was so much taken up with the dog, having to drag it along, that he hadn't time to notice I was following him!'

'Go on. What happened to get you so excited?' said Peter, impatiently.

'I'm coming to that,' said Colin. 'I followed them down Hartley Street and across Plain Square, and into a little dark alley that led between some big buildings. I went down the alley cautiously, because I couldn't see my way very well, and daren't put on my torch.'

'Was the man there?' asked Jack.

'Let me tell my story in my own way,' said Colin. 'I'm just coming to the strange part. I went right down the alley, and just as I was nearly at the end, I heard the man coming back. I knew it was him because he has the same kind of quick dry cough my grandpa has, and he was coughing as he came.'

'What did you do?' said Janet, as he stopped for breath.

'I squashed myself into a doorway,' said Colin, 'and the man walked right by without seeing me. But he hadn't got the dog with him. So I wondered where he had put it, and why he had gone down there and come straight back again. So I went to the end of the alley myself and switched on my torch.'

'And was the dog there?' asked Pam.

'No,' said Colin. 'The alley led into a little yard, surrounded entirely by high walls. It was a messy place, full of rubbish. I flashed my torch all round, expecting to see the dog somewhere, tied up, perhaps, or even in a kennel, but there wasn't a sign of it!'

'Where was it, then?' asked Janet, after a pause.

'That's what I don't know,' said Colin. 'I looked absolutely everywhere for that dog. I listened for him, I called softly, but no, not a growl, not a whine, not a movement. And when I tell you that there was no way out of that yard except by that narrow alley, you'll guess how puzzled I was. I mean, a dog can't just *disappear*, can it?'

'Woof!' said Scamper, exactly as if he was saying 'No!'

'I hunted all over that horrible yard,' said Colin. 'That's why I'm so dirty. And I cut my hand on some wire. But I tell you, there was no sign of that lovely bull-terrier, and no door or gate or anything for him to get out of. Then where was he? What had that man done with him, and why? It just beats me. I just *had* to come back and tell you.'

'There's something funny about this,' said

Peter. 'I vote we go to that yard tomorrow and explore it. If there is some hiding-place there for a dog, we'll find it!'

'What a pity George isn't in this too,' said Janet. 'Peter, do go to that hotel and tell that young man he's got to go and tell George's parents they're to let him join the Secret Seven again. He'll be so upset when he knows we may be mixed up in something odd again and he won't be there to share in it.'

'All right, we'll go tomorrow after school,' said Peter. 'And then we'll go and explore that yard!'

'Yes, dogs don't just disappear,' said Jack. 'I expect there's a kennel there, or something, that you didn't notice in the dark, Colin.'

'Pooh!' said Colin. 'I'll give you fifty pence out of my money-box if you find a kennel there. You just see!'

CHAPTER TEN

The young man at Starling's

SO, AFTER school the next afternoon, Colin, Jack and Peter set off to go to Starling's Hotel, to see if they could find the young man who had hauled George home the other night and caused him to leave the Secret Seven.

They discussed what to say to him. 'We'll tell him the marvellous things that the Secret Seven have done,' said Peter. 'He'll soon see that a Society that can do the things we've done would only have decent boys and girls as members. I might tell him to go and ask the police about us. They would stick up for us like anything, because we've helped them so much.'

At last they came to Starling's. It was rather a poor little hotel. There was a woman in the

hall, and Peter asked her politely if there was a young man staying there. If so, could they please speak to him?'

'What's his name?' asked the woman.

'We don't know,' said Peter.

'Well, what's he like?' said the woman, sounding impatient.

'We, we don't know that either,' said Peter, feeling foolish, and wishing that he had asked George for a description of the man. 'All we know is that he's young.'

'Oh well, I suppose it's Mr Taylor you want,' said the woman, ungraciously. 'He's the only young man staying here. Go into that room and I'll ask him to come and speak to you.'

They went into a tiny room and stood about

awkwardly. Soon a young man came in and eyed the three boys curiously. 'What do you want?' he said.

Peter explained. 'It's about George, our friend,' he said. 'The boy you caught the other night. You thought he was up to no good, but actually he was only putting in a bit of shadowing practice. He belonged to our Secret Society, you see, and we do all kinds of things. George's parents have told him he's not to belong, so . . .'

'Well, it's nothing to do with me,' said the young man. 'I can't do anything. He shouldn't play the fool.'

'He wasn't,' said Peter, warming up. 'I tell you, we're a very well-known society here, the police know us well; we've helped them many a time.'

'What rubbish!' said the young man.

'You ring up the Inspector and ask about us, then!' said Jack, indignantly.

The young man seemed rather astonished at this. He stared at Jack as if wondering whether to find out about them from the police or not.

'Well, whether you are friends with the police or not, I'm not having any more to do with your friend George, or whatever his name is,' said the young man. 'So that's that. He's got no right to shadow people, whether in play or not. Now, clear out all of you.'

Colin hadn't said a word. He had been

eyeing the young man closely, and Peter wondered why. Was he trying to do as the girls had done, and 'observe' someone closely so that he could describe him later?

As they went out, gloomy and resentful, a dog barked somewhere.

Colin turned to the young man. "Is that your dog barking?' he asked.

'What dog? No! I haven't got a dog. And it wouldn't be any good if I had,' said the young man. 'They're not allowed in this hotel.'

Colin said no more, and the three boys walked out of the little hotel. They said nothing till they were well beyond the gate.

'He's hateful!' burst out Peter. 'Horrible cold eyes and thin mouth! As soon as I saw him I knew he was the kind of person that likes to get people into trouble. We once had a horrid teacher at school who had a mouth just like that!'

'Colin, why didn't you help us?' said Jack, as they walked down the road. 'You never said a word, till you asked about the dog that barked. Did you *have* to be unfriendly like that? You might have backed us up.'

'Wait a minute, I'll soon tell you why,' said Colin, and then the others saw that he was bursting to say something. 'Let's get right out of sight and hearing of Starling's first.'

They walked on a few hundred yards, and then Colin spoke in a low voice.

'That fellow, that young man, *he was the same one I saw last night* with the dog that disappeared!'

Jack and Peter stopped in surprise. 'What! Are you sure? But you asked him if it was his dog that was barking, and he said no he hadn't a dog!' Peter blurted all this out in far too loud a voice. Colin was afraid the passers-by might hear and he nudged Peter's arm.

'Be quiet. This may be important. Don't let's give anything away.'

'It's very interesting,' said Peter. 'Let's go to that yard at once and explore. We know the young man is safely at Starling's. He won't disturb us.'

'Come on, then,' said Colin. 'Oh, *bother*! Here's Susie.'

And Susie it was, coming at them like a hurricane, all out of breath. 'Peter! I've heard that George isn't in the Secret Seven any more. Please, PLEASE let me in! Jack, tell Peter to let me be in.'

'Certainly *NOT*,' said all three boys at once. 'We've got a seventh member already, thank you,' said Peter, remembering Scamper thankfully.

'Oh, bother! I did hope I'd be in time,' said Susie, and sailed off at top speed.

'What *cheek*!' said Jack. 'Honestly, she's the limit. Come on, let's go to this yard before Susie thinks of following us. Of all the *cheek*!'

The three boys set off in the direction of the yard that Colin had told them about.

'Hartley Street first,' said Colin, 'then across Plain Square. We come to the poorer parts of the town then.'

It took them a quarter of an hour to get to Plain Square, for Starling's Hotel was away at the other end of the town. They crossed the square, and then Colin looked for the alleyway leading between high buildings.

'There seem to be two or three,' said Peter. 'Which one was it, Colin?'

Colin hesitated. 'It all looks so different in the daylight,' he said. 'I think it's that one. But I'll soon know when we get to the yard. I'll never forget that yard, rubbishy, dirty place it was!'

They chose an alley-way, and went down it. It came out into a small enclosure that had evidently been made into a playground for children. Some little girls were there, riding tricycles and pushing prams. They stared at the three boys.

'Not this one,' said Colin, and they went back down the alley. They chose the next one and went down that. 'I think this is the one,' said Colin. 'Here's the doorway I hid in to let the young man pass!'

They came to the end of the alley and Colin gave an exclamation. 'Yes! This is the yard. I recognise that pile of old boxes, and that broken-down rusty pram. This is where the man took the dog, disposed of it somewhere, and came back without it.'

The boys gazed round. High walls enclosed the little yard. A few dusty windows overlooked it, and Peter suddenly wondered if anyone would open a window and yell to them to clear out.

'Listen,' he said, in a low voice. 'We'd better be looking for our ball, or something, in case somebody gets suspicious of us and turns us away before we've discovered anything. Anyone got a ball?'

Colin had, a very small ping-pong ball, but it would do! He carefully dropped it in among some rubbish, and then the boys pretended to hunt for it. But really they were hunting for any place where a dog might have been put.

They turned that yard upside down, growing bolder as nobody disturbed them. It was a very quiet, lonely little yard, completely enclosed, with no outlet but the alley-way, and had obviously been used for a dumping place for old boxes, crates, broken crockery, sacks, sheets of cardboard and other things.

'Everything here but the dog!' said Peter at last. 'I think we've looked into every crate and box, and into every corner where a dog could be, though no dog would keep quiet if it heard us three rummaging about. There *must* be some outlet here besides that alley-way, an outlet big enough for a dog, anyway.'

They had moved every crate and box away from the walls, hoping to find some small door, but apparently the high walls contained no opening of any kind. It was a mystery!

Jack sat down on a big box in the middle of the yard to rest. Colin fell on him in one of his sudden silly fits, and began to wrestle with him, trying to get him off the box. Both boys fell over, and the box turned over too.

'Shut up,' said Peter, crossly. 'That box made quite a crash, turning over like that.'

Colin and Jack got up, brushing the dust off themselves, and grinning. Then Peter gave a cry. He clutched Jack's arm, and pointed down at his feet.'

'Look – see that? What about *that* for pushing a dog through?'

All three were now staring down at Jack's feet. He was standing on an iron lid, a perfectly round one that fitted over what must have been a coal-hole.

'It was under that box, well hidden,' said Peter, excited. 'About the only box we didn't move, I should think. But who would have thought a coal-hole was under it? We didn't really *think* of a coal-hole, anyhow! Get off it, Jack, and let's have a look at it.'

Jack stepped off the round lid, and they all knelt down to look closely at it. 'It's been moved recently,' said Peter. 'It's not as caked with dirt round the edges as it should be. I bet that bull-terrier was shoved through here, Colin; I bet he was!'

'But why push a lovely dog down through a coal-hole?' said Colin, puzzled. 'What an extraordinary thing to do! And it seems a bit odd to me to have a coal-hole in this little yard. No coal-cart can come up that alley-way.'

'But a coal-man with a sack of coal can, stupid!' said Peter. 'Can we get this lid up? I'd

75

like to peep down, and see if there's anything to be seen!'

It was an awkward thing to get up, besides being extremely heavy. Peter got very cross with it. But at last it was lifted, and shoved to one side. Then the boys all bent over eagerly, to look down. Their heads cracked together.

'I get first look,' said Peter, firmly. 'I'm the chief.' So the others let him look first.

He sat back, disappointed. 'Well, it's as dark and black as a, well, as a coal-hole!' he said. 'Can't see a single thing. Anyone got a torch?'

'I've still got mine on me,' said Colin, and got it out of his pocket. They shone it down the dark hole. But even the light of the torch showed them nothing. Certainly there was no sign of a dog!

There was no sign of coal or coke either. It looked just a dark, horrible, deep hole.

'Er – anyone like to jump down?' said Peter.

CHAPTER ELEVEN

The coal-hole

NOBODY WANTED to jump down in the least. For one thing, the hole wasn't very big – for another, the dark ground was a long way below – and for a third thing, who knew what might lie in wait for any daring boy dropping down through that hole!

'Well, I must say I think it would be rather silly to get down there, knowing as little as we do about this affair,' said Peter, at last. 'Do you suppose this is where the dog was pushed down, Colin?'

'I don't know,' said Colin, puzzled. 'The dog's not there now, anyway, dead or alive. The hole is empty. I suppose it's really an underground cellar, and may be quite big.

Anyway, what's the point of pushing a lovely dog down a coal-hole? It doesn't make sense to me.'

'We'd better put the lid back and go home,' said Peter. 'It's getting dark. I'm not sure I like this nasty lonely little yard now it's getting towards night-time!'

He took hold of the lid, but Colin stopped him. 'Wait a minute,' he said. 'I've got an idea.'

He put his head right down into the hole. Then he whistled. Colin had a very shrill, piercing whistle that usually went right through people's heads and made them angry. His shrill whistle sounded now, though it could not be very well heard up in the yard, because Colin's head was in the hole. It could be heard down in the cellar, though, for the piercing noise echoed round and round!

'What are you doing that for?' began Peter, angrily, but Jack guessed, and nudged him to be quiet. Colin was now listening, his head still down the hole. He heard something – what was it? Yes, there it came again. Then it stopped.

He took his head out, his eyes shining. 'The dog's down there somewhere all right,' he said. 'It heard my whistle, and I heard it barking, far away, somewhere, goodness knows where.'

'Gosh! Did you really?' said Peter, amazed.

'That was a really good idea of yours, Colin. Well, we now know for certain that the dog's down there, so that man must have pushed him into the hole. This is a mystery all right.'

'Yes. One that has sprung up all of a sudden, as mysteries usually do,' said Colin. 'What do we do next? We could get down the hole if we brought a rope-ladder, but we'll break our legs if we just try to *drop* down.'

There was a pause. The boys sat back on their bent knees and thought hard.

'The cellar must belong to one of these buildings,' said Jack, at last. 'But which one?

It might belong to any of these around us. The coal-hole is exactly in the centre of the yard.'

'I can't see that it matters which one,' said Peter.

'Well, it might,' said Jack. 'We could find out if any firm in these buildings is interested in dogs.'

'Well, I suppose that's an idea,' said Peter, doubtfully. 'Anyway, let's put this lid back now, and place the box over it. We don't want anyone to suspect we've come across part of their secret.'

They put back the lid as quietly as they could, and dragged the box across it. Now it was as well hidden as when they had first come into the yard.

'It's almost dark now,' said Peter. 'We'd better get back home. My mother will be wondering where I am – and oh, bother – I've not done my homework yet. It's awfully difficult to swot at French verbs when you're thinking out a mystery all the time.'

'Look!' said Jack, as they turned to leave the yard. 'Look! Only one of these buildings has a lit window. Do you suppose the coal-cellar belongs to that one? Do you think there's anyone looking after that bull-terrier? He must be scared stiff if he's all by himself.'

The boys stared up at the lit window.

'It's the building on the left,' said Peter. 'It will be just round the corner of the block. Let's go that way and see what firm uses it. It might be a help, though, of course, the lit window may have nothing whatever to do with the mystery!'

They left the yard cautiously, went down the dark alley-way, and out into the street. They walked round the block, and came to the building that they thought must have shown the lit window. Colin switched his torch on to the dirty brass plate in the main doorway.

'Alliance of Callinated Sack Manufacturers!' he read. 'What on earth does that mean? Anyway, by the look of the building, the sack manufacturers must have gone west long ago. What a desolate, dirty place! It hasn't had a touch of paint for years!'

'It may be one of the buildings that the Council plan to pull down,' said Jack. 'I know some of them round about here are being

pulled down, they're so old. Come on, let's go.'

'Look!' said Peter suddenly, and pulled the others to one side. 'The door's opening!'

Sure enough it was. The boys stood quietly in the shadows, waiting. Someone came out and shut the door softly. He went down the few steps into the street. He kept close to the wall as he walked along, a tall, stooping man.

With one accord the boys followed, their

rubber shoes making no sound. They knew that a lamp-post was round the corner. Perhaps they could see this man more clearly in the lamp-light. Who was he?

'We'll shadow him!' whispered Peter. 'Come on.'

CHAPTER TWELVE

Two interesting encounters

THE MAN came into the light of the street lamp, but only for a second. Peter tried to take in everything at one glance. He suddenly thought that Janet would have been very, very good at that!

The man went past the lamp, and into the darkness again.

Couldn't see very much, really, thought Peter. He had his hat pulled so well down over his face. He seems to limp a bit. Bother, I'd never recognise him again!

The man got along pretty quickly. He was making for the bus-stop. It was easy for the boys to shadow him, because now other people were walking in the street too.

'He's making for the bus-stop,' said Colin.

'We'll see which bus he catches. Shall we get on it, and look at him more carefully?'

'Yes,' said Peter, forgetting the lateness of the evening, forgetting his homework, in fact forgetting everything except for the excitement of the moment. They were on the track of a new mystery. How could anyone stop in the middle of it and go home!

The man made for the second of the two buses that were standing at the stop.

'It's the bus for Pilberry,' said Peter. 'Come on, we'll get on too.'

The man put out his hand to the bus-rail and swung himself up. Other people followed. The boys began to get on too, but the conductor put out his arm.

'Sorry,' he said. 'Full up!'

He rang the bell, and the bus rumbled off.

'Bother!' said Peter, disappointed. 'We might have been able to shadow him all the way home.'

'Well, I don't expect he's anything to do with the dog affair, really,' said Colin. 'We might have gone on a real wild-goose chase, and found he was just a harmless old businessman, catching a bus home.'

'Peter! Colin! Did you notice his hand?' said Jack, in a voice suddenly bubbling with excitement. 'When he put it out to take hold of the bus-rail?'

'No. Why?' said both boys at once.

'Well, he had two fingers missing, and the hand was crooked,' said Jack. 'Don't you remember Janet's report, don't you re—'

'Gosh, yes!' said Peter. 'That man she described getting off the train from Pilberry, at the station on Saturday morning! Hat well pulled down over his eyes, he walked a bit lame, a funny hand . . .'

'And very square shoulders,' said Colin. 'It all fits. He's the same man. But wait a bit, there's nothing extraordinary about us seeing the same man as Janet saw, is there? I mean, it's only just chance, and doesn't *mean* anything.'

'No, you're right. It doesn't really mean anything,' said Jack, his excitement fading. 'It just seemed strange, that's all. Perhaps we're making a mountain out of a mole-hill – he's just an ordinary person going home.'

They turned to walk across the square again, and passed the little alley-way that led to the yard. Someone came out of it briskly, and almost bumped into them.

It was too dark to see what the man was like, but he soon passed under a lamp-post, and something swinging from his hand caught Jack's eye.

'Look, a dog-lead,' he said, in a low voice. 'But no dog! It's the same man who lives at Starling's Hotel.'

'The one I saw with the dog yesterday!' said Colin, excited. 'What's he doing here again? Has he taken another dog into that yard and pushed it down the coal-hole? Gosh! This is all very peculiar, isn't it? What *is* going on?'

They went on, keeping well behind the young man. He went round a corner, and vanished from sight. The boys went round the corner too, and then got a sudden shock.

The young man came out from a doorway as they passed and caught hold of Colin and Peter by the shoulder. He flashed a torch in their faces.

'Ha – it's you three, is it?' he said. 'Members

of the famous Secret Shadowing Gang, or whatever you call yourselves! I *thought* you were following me! Look here, I took that fourth boy, what's his name, George, to his parents, and got him punished for this idiotic following of people at night. And I've a good mind to take you to the police, the three of you, and hand you over for making yourselves a nuisance by doing the same thing!'

'All right,' said Peter, at once. 'Take us to the police. We don't mind. Go on, take us!'

The young man hesitated. He evidently hadn't thought that Peter would challenge him like that. The boys stood there, scowling. Colin suddenly asked a question.

'Where's your dog?'

'What do you mean? I haven't a dog!' said the young man, angrily. 'You seem to have got dogs on your mind. You asked me that when you came to see me this afternoon.'

'Well, why the dog lead, if you haven't a dog?' said Colin, pointing to it.

'Look here, who do you think you are, asking foolish questions, interfering, following people? And what's all this about dogs? What's on your mind?'

The boys didn't answer that question. 'Are you going to take us to the police or not?' said Jack. 'We're ready, if you are. You can tell them anything you like. But we might tell them a few things too.'

'Pah!' said the young man, looking as if he would like to lash out with the dog-lead at the boys. 'I've had enough of you. Clear off home, and don't let me see you again!'

Off he went with angry steps. 'Well!' said Peter, staring after him. 'He certainly didn't dare to take us to the police – but why? What a very puzzling peculiar young man!'

All these exciting happenings made it necessary to call another Secret Seven meeting as soon as possible. The members simply *must* talk over everything, and try to sort things out. So, before afternoon school on Thursday, Peter called a half-hour meeting.

'What a pity George is out of it!' said Janet. 'He would so love to hear all that's happening.'

'I don't see why we can't tell him,' said Jack. 'He can't come to the meeting, of course, but I can't for the life of me see why we shouldn't tell him all that happens. After all, it was *his* first shadowing that began all this!'

'Well, he isn't a member,' said Peter, who liked the rules to be kept. 'We ought not to let anyone but the seven members know what we're doing. Otherwise we're not a Secret Society.'

'Woof,' said Scamper, thumping his tail on the floor of the shed. He seemed to think that he had to make some remark about everything, now that he was a proper member.

'Let's put it to the vote,' said Janet. 'I like rules being kept too, but it isn't George's fault he's out of this. I feel as if he really does still belong to us.'

So they put it to the vote, and fortunately

everyone was of the same mind. George should certainly be told everything that happened. It would make up to him a little for being out of the Society. Scamper said 'Woof' so loudly when he was asked that everyone took it for 'Yes'. So it was solemnly recorded that the whole of the Secret Seven thought it right and proper to keep George up to date in the doings of the Society.

A very exciting discussion was held. Everyone wanted to talk at once, so Peter became very strict and insisted that only one person should speak at a time.

It was decided that the old man, who came out of the lighted-window building and got on the bus, was the same one that Janet had seen at the station.

'He probably lives at Pilberry,' said Janet. 'I saw him getting off the train from Pilberry, and you saw him getting on the bus for Pilberry. Though I can't see that it's at all important to know where he lives. He may not have anything to do with this affair at all.'

'That's what we said,' said Jack. 'But we feel he *might* have something to do with it, so we'll keep our eyes open for him and his doings. Your description was so good, Janet, that we all recognised him for the man you saw!'

Janet was pleased, Pam and Barbara wished heartily that they had not had giggling fits at the bus-stop, but had noticed people as carefully as Janet had. Well, they would do better the next time!

The coal-hole was well and truly discussed.

'It's pretty certain that for some reason that young man takes dogs there secretly at night, and puts them through the hole,' said Colin. 'Then he leaves them. Do you suppose somebody is down there, waiting to receive them? I mean, somebody *must* look after them, surely?'

'Yes. But WHY are they taken there and hidden?' said Jack. 'That's what *I* want to know. I feel sorry for the dogs. We ought to get the RSPCA after them. It's cruel to push dogs through coal-holes and leave them there in the darkness. For all we know they have no food or drink.'

'There wouldn't be any sense in starving them,' said Peter. 'The dogs must be stolen ones. That's quite clear. We've seen one of

them. You, Colin, said it was a fine bull-terrier, so it was probably a very valuable dog, and would fetch a good deal of money.'

'Yes, and the one that man must have taken last night, when we bumped into him, would have been some other kind of valuable dog, too,' said Jack. 'Gosh! Do you suppose that cellar is full of pure-bred dogs, all stolen? We'll have to do something about this!'

'Poor dogs!' said Pam. 'What happens to them down in the cellar? I do, do hope there's somebody there to see to them.'

There was a silence. Everyone was thinking the same thing. Something had got to be done about those dogs! Somehow that cellar had to be explored.

Colin, Pam and Jack began to talk loudly at the same time, and Peter rapped on the box in front of him.

'Silence! I've said you've got to talk one at a time. Has anyone any suggestions? Pam, what have you got to say?'

'Well, I've got rather a good idea,' said Pam. 'Can't we look up the Lost and Found advertisements in the newspapers, and see if many dogs are advertised as lost or stolen?'

'Yes. *Very* good idea,' said Peter, and Pam felt pleased. 'We'll do that.'

'And couldn't we go to the police station and look at the notices outside too?' asked Jack.

'They often have posters giving particulars of lost animals.'

'Excellent,' said Peter. 'Any more ideas?'

'We *must* explore that cellar,' said Colin. 'I did wonder if we should try to get into that building with the lighted window and see if its cellar led to that coal-hole – but we might get into awful trouble if we got in there. Isn't it called "Breaking in" or something?'

'Yes. We can't do that,' said Peter, firmly. 'We can't *possibly* do wrong things in order to put something right. We'll have to explore the coal-hole, but I can't see that it matters doing that. Now, we'd better make plans.'

'Everybody's got to do something!' said Jack. 'Give us our jobs, Peter, and we'll do them. Hurrah – the Secret Seven is going full speed again!'

CHAPTER THIRTEEN

Jobs for everyone

PETER GAVE each one of them a job to do. 'Pam and Barbara, hunt through every paper you can get hold of and find out if there are many valuable dogs advertised as lost or stolen,' he said.

'Yes, Peter,' said the two girls.

'And mind you do your job properly this time,' said Peter, sternly. 'Janet, you can go and look outside the police-station and see if there are any notices there, and, as it's fairly near George's house, you can go and tell him all the latest news. He didn't come to school today, because he has a cough, so he'll be glad to see you.'

'Yes, Peter,' said Janet, pleased.

'And you, Colin, and you, Jack, will come with me and Scamper to the coal-hole tonight,' said Peter, dropping his voice, and sounding suddenly serious and determined. 'Colin, bring that rope-ladder you've got. It will be just right for dropping down into the hole, it's not too long. Bring torches, both of you, and wear rubber shoes.'

'Yes, Peter,' said the boys, looking and feeling very thrilled indeed. What an adventure!

'Woof-woof-woof,' said Scamper.

'He said "Yes, Peter," too!' said Janet. 'You understand every word we're saying, don't you, Scamper, darling?'

'Today's Thursday,' said Pam. 'Have you

1 PAM AND BARBARA
2 JANET
3 COLIN, JACK, PETER

forgotten that you three boys are going to Ronnie's party, all of you? You can't do anything much today.'

'Bother! I'd forgotten that!' said Peter. 'We'll have to explore the coal-hole on Friday, then. But you girls can get on with your jobs all right. Now, I think that's about all, so we'll go. We'll just be in good time for school.'

They all went out of the shed, Scamper too, wagging his tail importantly. Pam and Barbara decided to go after school to the public library, where there were many papers they could read for Lost and Found advertisements. So, much to the librarian's astonishment, they seated themselves there, with copies of the daily papers and of the local papers too, around them.

They made some interesting discoveries. 'Look, Pam,' said Barbara, pointing with her finger to two advertisements. '"Lost or stolen, pedigree greyhound." "Lost or stolen, purebred bull-terrier." Why, that might be the very one Colin saw! It gives names and addresses here, both in our county.'

'I've found an interesting advertisement too,'

said Pam. 'See – "Lost on Monday, 16th, a beautiful pedigree Saluki. Answers to name of Sally." That's in our county too. It looks as if somebody is at work, stealing pedigree dogs!'

'Here's another,' said Barbara. '"Believed stolen, pure-bred Alsatian, well trained, answers to name of Kip." Goodness! Suppose the boys find them all down that coal-hole!'

'What do you suppose the thief does with them?' said Pam.

'Sells them again, of course. They would be worth a lot of money,' said Barbara. 'Or they might claim the reward offered. See, there's a reward of one hundred pounds for anyone finding the Alsatian!'

'I wonder how Janet will get on, looking at

the police notices!' said Pam. 'Anyway, we've done well this time. Peter can't tick us off again!'

Janet couldn't go to the police-station till the following day. She gobbled down her midday dinner and raced off. She meant to look at the police notices, and then go and see George and tell him all the latest news.

There was only one notice about dogs, and that was to say that dogs found worrying sheep would be shot. Janet hoped with all her heart that Scamper would never do such a silly thing. She didn't think he would, because her father owned a lot of sheep, and Scamper was used to them. It would be so dreadful if he was shot.

She glanced at the next notice. It described a man that the police wanted to find. Janet read it with interest.

'John Wilfrid Pace, aged 71. Small and bent. Bald, with shaggy eyebrows and beard. Very hoarse voice. Shuffles badly when walking. Scar across the right cheek.'

'I should know *him* all right if I saw him!'

said Janet to herself, picturing a bent little man, bald and bearded, scarred on the face. 'Now I really must go and see George, or I'll be late for school.'

George was delighted to see Janet. He was perfectly all right except for a cough, but his mother was not going to let him go back to school until Monday.

'I've come to tell you all the latest news of the Secret Seven,' said Janet. 'Can anyone overhear us? We know you're not a member now, but we all voted that you should know what's going on. And there's plenty to tell you, George. It's all very, very exciting!'

So it was, and Janet told everything very well indeed. When she left George, he felt rather down in the dumps. All this going on and I'm not in it! he thought.

Then an idea came into his head. 'Well – why *shouldn't* I be in it? Why shouldn't I go to that coal-hole, and watch the others going down? They needn't even know I'm there! I can find it all right. Yes, I'll go. Look out, Secret Seven, I'm coming too, though you won't see me! Hurrah!'

CHAPTER FOURTEEN

Down the coal-hole!

RONNIE'S PARTY was a good one, and the three boys and Janet enjoyed themselves thoroughly. They quite forgot the exciting affair they were mixed up in, as they played all kinds of games.

But one game reminded them of the Secret Seven doings! Ronnie's mother suddenly came in with a tray of all kinds of things. 'Now, look well, everybody!' she said. 'There are twenty things here. I am going to find out which of you has the best powers of observation! Look well for one minute, and then I shall take the tray away, and you must each write down what you saw on the tray, as many as you can!'

You can guess who won that competition –

Janet! She remembered all twenty, and Peter was very proud of her.

'I believe you belong to a secret society, Janet,' said Ronnie's mother, giving her a box of chocolates as a prize. 'You must be one of its best members!'

That reminded the three boys of the exciting thing they were to do the next night. Down the coal-hole they would go, and what would they find there?

There was no time for a proper meeting before Friday night, so Janet, Pam and Barbara hurriedly told Peter what they had or had not found out about lost or stolen dogs. Peter was very interested indeed, especially when he heard that most of them were from their own county.

'That rather looks as if the thieves have their quarters in the county too,' he said. 'And if so, it may be down that coal-hole! I'd like to pay back that nasty young man for getting George into trouble. I'm sure he's mixed up in this!'

It was dark about seven o'clock. The three boys and Scamper met at the end of Peter's road, and set off together. Colin had his rope-ladder, and they all had their torches. They felt very excited.

It was a dark night, and a slight drizzle was falling. The boys turned up their coat collars. They went cautiously, in case that young man should turn up again out of some corner. They didn't like him. In fact each boy was secretly afraid of him. There was something horrid about his cold eyes and thin, cruel mouth that not one of them liked.

They went down Hartley Street and across Plain Square. A bus rumbled by and a few cars.

They came near to the alley-way. 'Do you suppose that man's coming with another dog tonight?' whispered Jack. 'We'd better keep a sharp look-out in case he does. It wouldn't do for him to find us getting down the coal-hole!'

DOWN THE COAL-HOLE!

'Well, you had better keep watch while we two get down,' said Peter. 'Then as soon as we're down you can make a run for the hole and get down yourself. I only hope that man *doesn't* come – we'd be nicely trapped if he did. He's only got to pop on the lid and we're prisoners. We couldn't possibly lift up that heavy lid from inside.'

This was not at all a nice thought. They went along even more cautiously, keeping a look-out for the young man. But there was no one to be seen near the alley-way. The boys went quietly down it and came into the yard. It was pitch-dark there.

They stood and listened for a while, with Scamper silent beside them. If the man was there they might hear a slight movement, or even breathing. But they heard nothing at all. It seemed quite safe to switch on torches and go across to the coal-hole.

Peter flashed his torch round quickly. The yard was deserted, dirty as ever, and very quiet. There was not even the lighted window to see.

They moved the box that hid the coal-hole and heaved off the heavy lid, and then Peter flashed his torch down. Nothing there but blackness and dirt. Colin undid the little rope-ladder he carried and let it drop slowly down into the coal-hole, rung by rung. Scamper watched it going down with much interest.

They peered down. Yes, it reached the bottom

nicely. Colin fastened the top end carefully to a nearby stone post.

'Now, Jack, you go to the entrance of the alley and keep guard till we're down,' whispered Peter. 'Come as soon as you hear a low whistle.'

Jack sped off obediently. Colin said he would go down first. So down he climbed, rung by rung, till he came to the bottom. He flashed his torch round. He was in a big coal-cellar. His feet crunched a little as he stepped here and there, and he guessed that there was still coke or coal dust on the floor.

'I'm coming now,' whispered Peter. 'Look out, I'm bringing Scamper too!' Down he came, and soon stood beside Colin. He remembered Jack, and sent a low whistle to tell him he could come.

Soon they heard Jack's feet above, and then he came down too, grinning in delight. They were all very excited, Peter flashed his torch all round.

'Now, there must be a way out of this cellar. Look, is that a door over there?'

'Yes,' said Jack. 'That probably leads into

the other cellars or basements. We'd better go cautiously – and listen hard as we go.'

'Nobody saw us go down, that's one good thing!' said Peter, thankfully.

But he was wrong. Somebody did see them go down. It is true that he could hardly make them out in the darkness, but he heard their low voices and knew what was happening! Who was it? George, of course!

George had done what he had made up his mind to do! He had found the yard with the coal-hole, and he was hiding to watch what happened. Somehow or other, Secret Seven member or not, George was going to be in on this!

CHAPTER FIFTEEN

Underground happenings

THE THREE boys down in the coal-hole were now carefully opening the door they had seen. Scamper was at Peter's heels, as excited as they were. Peter wished he didn't pant quite so loudly, but Scamper couldn't help that!

The door creaked as it was opened. There

was no light beyond. Peter cautiously flashed his torch on and off. A passage lay before him, leading to a few steps. A closed door was at the top of the steps.

The boys went along the passage and up the few steps and then turned the handle of the door. Would it be locked? No, it wasn't. It opened towards them, and Peter peered round the crack. Still there was darkness in front of them. He flashed his torch round.

Now they were in the main cellars that lay under the big building. They stretched here and there, low-roofed, with brick pillars standing up from floor to roof at intervals.

A noise came to Scamper's ears, and he listened, head on one side. Peter saw him listening, and listened too. But he could hear nothing. Scamper's ears were sharper than his.

They moved forward very cautiously, stopping every now and again to listen. It was very weird to be so far under a building, in the pitch darkness and loneliness of these vast cellars. They smelt strange too – musty and old and damp.

They came to another door – a wooden one

– and now Scamper began to get very excited. Peter had difficulty in preventing him from barking. And then, as they opened the stout wooden door, they heard what Scamper heard!

It was the noise of whining dogs! Scamper whined too when he heard, and wanted to dash through the door. Then came a barking and a yapping. Then more whining.

'There *are* dogs shut up here,' whispered Peter. 'We were right. Go carefully now, for goodness' sake.'

They came to a long, narrow cellar, where a faint light glowed from a glass bulb. On one side was a wooden bench, on which cages were set. In them were five or six dogs, their eyes gleaming red in the faint light.

Nobody was there with the dogs. They gazed warily and snarled as the three boys came quietly near, but when Scamper gave an excited, friendly whine, they whined too, pawing at their cages in excitement.

'They've got water and food,' whispered Peter. 'Oh, look, there's the lovely car-sick poodle we saw in that car, Jack, do you remember? We saw it when we were doing a bit of practice, hiding by the road in a spyhole, watching people go by. I'm sure it's the same poodle.'

'Yes. It is,' said Jack. 'Colin, there's a bull-terrier, see? He's the same one you saw with that young man, I suppose?'

Colin nodded. He was very fond of dogs, and he was already making friends with these, allowing them to lick his hand through the wires of the cages.

'There's a greyhound, and a magnificent Alsatian!' said Peter. 'I bet those are the ones the girls read about in the papers as lost or stolen. And here's a Dalmatian – hello, Spots! You're a beauty, aren't you?'

The dogs were now all very friendly to the boys, partly because they had a dog with them who was friendly too. Peter stood and looked at the dogs, wondering what to do next.

'Should we set them free from their cages, tie them together with rope and see if we can get them out of the coal-hole?' he said.

'Don't be silly!' said Colin. 'They'd never go up the rope-ladder – and I bet they'd begin to fight if we set them free.'

'Listen, somebody's coming!' said Jack, suddenly, and Scamper gave a warning growl. The boys went into the shadows and waited.

They saw an old bent man shuffling along, carrying a lantern. His head shone in the faint radiance of the electric light above, for he was quite bald. He had a small dog with him, a mongrel of some kind, and he talked to it as he came in a curious, hoarse voice like a creaking gate!

'Come on, Tinks. We'll see if all the lords and ladies are all right. They don't think nothing of the likes of you and me, but we don't care, do we?'

The little dog trotted beside him, and they came to the cages. The old man went on talking in his creaking voice, staring at the caged dogs.

'Well, my high-and-mighty ones, my lords and ladies, you're worse off than little Tinks here. You've lost your own masters, but he's got his. You may be worth your weight in gold, for all I know, but you'd give all you've got for a nice long walk, wouldn't you? Well, Tinks goes for two each day. Tell 'em, Tinks, tell 'em.'

But Tinks was not listening. He had smelt

strange smells, the smells of the three boys and the golden spaniel, Scamper! In a trice he was over beside them, barking madly.

The old man held up his lantern and peered at them. 'What, more visitors?' he creaked.

'Come to see the lords and ladies, have you? Wait now, you're only lads!'

Peter came out from the shadows with Jack and Colin. He didn't feel at all afraid of this strange old man.

'Where did these dogs come from?' he said. 'Who brought them here? Who do they belong to? What are you doing with them?'

The old man gave him a helpless look.

'Them dogs, why, they comes and they goes,' he said. 'They comes and they goes. They comes in at that hole and—'

But whatever he said next was quite drowned by a sudden yelping and barking by the dogs. They had heard somebody else coming. Who was it this time?

''Ere comes the Guvnor,' said the old man, and chuckled drily. 'Now you'll be in trouble. Likely he'll lock you up in them cages!'

CHAPTER SIXTEEN

Unpleasant surprises

SOMEBODY CAME up out of the shadows very suddenly and quietly. The boys swung round at his voice.

'And what are *you* doing here?'

It was the tall, stooping man they had seen coming out of the building and getting on the

bus! Yes, hat well pulled down, squared shoulders, odd hand! They couldn't see his face even now, under the shade of his black hat.

The boys, taken by surprise, didn't know what to say. The man suddenly opened a nearby cage, and spoke loudly.

'Guard them, Kip.'

The enormous Alsatian leapt out, went to the boys and glared at them, snarling and showing his teeth. Scamper shrank back, afraid. The boys didn't like it at all, either. They didn't dare to move a step.

The man laughed. 'That's right. Keep still. See my hand with two fingers off? Well, that's what an Alsatian did to me when I moved while he was guarding me!'

The boys said nothing. Peter felt wild with himself. They had thought themselves so clever, getting down to explore these cellars and see what they could find, and now here they were, trapped, and guarded by the fiercest Alsatian he had ever seen. He hoped and hoped that Scamper would not do anything silly. Kip would gobble him up in a mouthful.

The man fired questions at them. 'How did

you come here? What for? Does anyone know you are here? Do you know the kind of things that happen to boys who poke their noses into things that are no concern of theirs? You don't? Then you soon will!'

He gave a sudden sharp order to the bald old man, who was muttering to himself in his creaking voice. 'Got your keys? Then lock these boys up in the cages. Kip, bring them here.'

Kip rounded up the boys as if they had been sheep, and hustled them in front of the man. Then one by one the Alsatian propelled each of them into a cage, snarling if they resisted. The old bald man locked them in, chortling to himself. Colin saw there was a scar across his face as the man looked up at him. There was no doubt about it, he was the old man that Janet had read about in the police notice! But not one of them could tell the police that the fellow was here, because they were all well and truly locked up.

The dogs were roaming about, growling and uneasy. The stooping man had them under control, though, and one sharp word from him

was obeyed at once by any dog. He stood in front of the cages mockingly. Scamper was not in a cage, but crouched outside Peter's frightened and puzzled.

'I'm going now,' said the tall man to the little bald fellow. 'I'm taking the dogs in the car.

You won't see me again. It's too dangerous here now. You don't need to know anything if anyone comes asking questions. Just play the idiot – that should be easy for you!'

'I'm afraid of the police,' creaked the old man.

'Well, hide away in the cellars,' said the other. 'It's a warren of a place. No one will ever find you. Let these kids out in twenty-four hours' time. I'll be well away by then, so it doesn't matter what kind of tale they tell! They don't know anything, anyway.'

'We do!' said Peter, boldly. 'We know that all these dogs are stolen. We know that this bald man is wanted by the police. We know the young man who brings the dogs here for you! We know you use the building above this cellar for your headquarters. We know—'

The tall man limped over to Peter's cage. For one moment the boy saw his furious, gleaming eyes and was afraid. Scamper thought he was about to harm Peter, and he flew at him and bit him hard on the ankle!

The man gave an exclamation and kicked out at Scamper. He caught him in the mouth, and the dog fled away yelping, and was lost in the shadows.

Then the man was gone, and with him went the dogs, cowed and obedient. He obviously had some extraordinary control over them – perhaps he had been a dog trainer, Peter thought. The old bald man laughed hoarsely at the frightened faces of the three boys in the cages, and his little mongrel dog sat down beside him with his mouth open as if he was laughing too.

'Boys! I don't like boys! Nasty tormenting creatures. I always said they ought to be shut up in cages!' He gave a creaking laugh. 'And now here you are, locked in my cages, and nobody knows where you are. Shall I tell you something, young sirs? If the police come after me and take me, I'll not tell them about you. I'll say to myself, "What, you'll take poor old John Pace and shut him up? Aha! Then I won't tell you about those boys!"'

He went off into a cackle of laughter, and then set off with his little mongrel at his heels. The boys were silent for a moment and then Peter spoke.

'We're properly caught. Goodness knows how long we'll be in this dark, horrible, smelly place. I wonder where Scamper's gone. He can't get up that rope-ladder by himself, or he'd go home and get help. I hope he's not hurt.'

'Sh! Listen! There's somebody else coming!' said Colin. 'I heard something, I'm sure. Gosh! I hope it's not that horrible young man. It would be just our luck if he came along with another dog for the other man!'

There was a pattering noise as well as cautious footsteps. Was it that young man and a dog? The three boys held their breath as the footsteps came nearer and nearer. Then a torch suddenly flashed out on the cages!

CHAPTER SEVENTEEN

Good old George!

A FAMILIAR voice came to the three boys' ears. 'Peter! Colin! Jack! Whatever are you doing in those cages?'

'Why, it's George! George, is it really you?' cried Peter, joyfully. 'And Scamper! Is Scamper hurt?'

'No. But what on earth has happened?' said George, in the greatest amazement, as he gazed at the boys in the cages.

'How did *you* get in here?' demanded Jack. 'I was never so surprised in all my life as when I heard your voice.'

'I knew you were coming here tonight, because Janet told me,' explained George. 'And I thought I'd come too, even though I didn't belong to the Secret Seven any more. I thought I'd just watch. I saw you go down, and gosh! I did want to join you. I was hiding in that yard.'

'Well, I never!' said Peter. 'What made you come down into the cellars, then?'

'I waited ages for you to come back, and you didn't,' said George. 'And then I suddenly heard old Scamper whining like anything down in the hole. So I hopped out of my hiding-place and went down the ladder to him. That's all. But WHY are you in those cages? Can't you get out?'

'No,' groaned Peter. 'It's too long a story to tell you, George. You must go and get the police. Wait, though, look round first and

see if that old man has hung the cage keys anywhere!'

George flashed his torch here and there, and gave a sudden exclamation.

'Yes, here are some keys, on this nail. I'll try them in the padlocks.'

He tried first one and then another in the padlock on Peter's cage door, and there was a sudden click!

'Oh good!' said Peter, as the lock opened. He pushed open the cage door. Soon the others were out too. They were most relieved.

'Now quick, we'll get the police,' said Peter. 'Come on, Scamper, old thing. Fancy you going and whining to George like that! I suppose you knew he was hiding in that yard, though *we* didn't!'

They hurried through the cellars, and came to the coal-hole. Up the rope-ladder they went. They pulled up the ladder and then picked their way through the yard, their hearts beating quickly. Scamper was very pleased with himself indeed. He felt that he had been a first-class member of the Secret Seven!

The four boys and the dog caused quite a

sensation at the police-station, arriving dirty
and full of excitement. The police sergeant was
there. He knew them, and was far more willing
to listen to their extraordinary story than the old
policemen would have been.

They poured it out, and the sergeant called a
most interested policeman to take down notes.

The story went on and on, taken up first
by one boy, then another. 'Stolen dogs – the
coal-hole – the young man and the dog that
vanished – the cellars below – the strange bald

caretaker who looked after the dogs – yes, he's the man you've got a notice about outside the police station. The tall, stooping man – yes, he's got away. He's taken the dogs – in a car, he said.'

'I bet he's taken them in that car we saw the sick poodle in the other day!' said Peter, suddenly. 'I bet he has. Wait – I've got the number here. If you could find that car, sir, you'd probably find all the dogs *and* that man too! Gosh! I can't find the bit of paper I wrote down the number on.' He fumbled anxiously in all his pockets but the paper was not there.

'Think of the number. Try hard!' urged the sergeant. 'This is important. If we get that number, we can send out details, and the car will be stopped in a few minutes, no matter where it is. Think.'

'I know the *number*,' groaned Peter. 'It was 188. But what were the letters?'

'I know! Pretty Sick Dog!' cried Jack, suddenly remembering.

The sergeant looked astonished. 'Pretty Sick Dog?' he said. 'I don't follow.'

'PSD,' grinned Jack. 'The dog was sick, so we said the car letters must stand for Pretty Sick Dog – see? That's it – PSD 188.'

'Telephone that number to the patrol cars,' said the sergeant to the policeman. 'Quick now! We'll get him yet. My word, we've been after these dog stealers for months. That fellow's a wonder at getting any dog to come to him, then he pops it into his car and away it goes. He hands it to somebody else, who passes it on again—'

'Yes, they go to the young man who lives at

Starling's Hotel!' said Peter. 'We know he put a dog down the coal-hole to the old caretaker with the bald head and scar. You could get that young man too, Sergeant. He doesn't know about the happenings tonight! And you can get the caretaker as well. You've only to send men down the coal-hole into the cellar and up into the building above.'

The sergeant stared at Peter in awe. 'I haven't time to ask you how you know all these remarkable things,' he said. 'Car numbers – young men at Starling's – stolen dogs and their hiding place – wanted men – I just haven't time. I can't understand it.'

'Oh, well, we belong to the best Secret Society in the world, you know,' said Peter, unable to help boasting. 'We are always on the lookout for things to happen. Actually, we weren't *really* on the lookout this time. We rather *made* them happen, I think.'

The sergeant laughed. 'Well, make a few more happen. Now you'd better get home. It's late. I'll come and see you tomorrow. So long, and many, many thanks!'

CHAPTER EIGHTEEN

The jigsaw is finished

EIGHT WORRIED and amazed fathers and mothers heard the strange story of the stolen dogs when the four boys at last got home, very late, and full of excitement. Janet heard Peter come in, and flew downstairs from her bed, anxious to hear everything.

'What! You found the dogs in cages! And oh, how extraordinary that the man I read about on that police notice was there! Oh, goodness, were you really locked up in the dog-cages? And did Scamper, dear, darling, brave old Scamper, go and fetch George to your rescue? Scamper, you are one of the very, very best Secret Seven members!'

'Woof!' said Scamper, proudly, and sat up very straight.

Janet laughed at the Pretty Sick Dog business. So did everybody. It struck them as very funny. The whole adventure seemed rather extraordinary now it was over. It was a curious mystery, a strange little adventure, that had really grown out of the 'job' and 'practices' that Peter had set all the members to do.

'In fact, we each had one bit of a jigsaw puzzle, and when we found they fitted together, we saw what the picture was!' said Peter. 'We each did our bit, even old George.'

Next morning there was a Secret Seven meeting, of course, and will you believe it, George was there too, beaming all over his face.

'I say, can I come in?' he said, when he arrived, and banged on the door. 'Oh, the password, it's still "Beware", isn't it? It was a very good one for this adventure, wasn't it? We all had to "Beware" like anything. I guessed you'd have a Secret Seven meeting this morning, so I've come too. My father says I can be a member again if you'll have me!'

'Oh, George!' cried everyone in delight, and Peter dragged him in at once. 'Did he really? Why? Because we've done such a good job again, and you helped?'

'Yes. You see, the Inspector and the sergeant both came to ask me a few questions, and they told Dad and Mother that all the Secret Seven were quite remarkable people, and Dad never said a word about having had me turned out! And after the policeman had gone, Dad said "All right, George. I give in. You can belong again. You can go and tell the Secret Seven to make you a member again." So here I am.'

'We solemnly make you a member, George,' said Janet in delight. 'Scamper, we told you you were only temporary, didn't we? So you won't mind George taking your place. But you

134

were very, very good as a member, Scamper.
Wasn't he, everybody?'

They all agreed heartily, and Scamper looked
pleased and surprised to have so many pats and
kind words. He gave a little whine as if to say
'Well, what about a biscuit too?'

And Janet, always ready to understand his
smallest whine, at once produced a big biscuit
from a tin! 'You deserve it,' she said. 'If you
hadn't gone to fetch George to the rescue last
night, Peter and Colin and Jack would still be
locked up in the dog-cages!'

'Gosh! So we would,' said Peter. 'Hello,
who's this coming?'

The big kindly face of the Inspector looked
through the little window, with the sergeant
alongside.

'We don't know the password,' said the
Inspector, sorrowfully. 'Or we'd say it and
come in.'

'It's "Beware"!' said Peter, grinning and flung
open the door. 'We'll soon have to choose a
new one, so it doesn't matter telling you.'

'Have you got any news?' asked Colin
eagerly.

'Oh yes, that's why we came to find you,' said the Inspector. 'We thought you ought to know the results of the good work done by the remarkable Society you belong to!'

'Oh good – tell us!' said Janet.

'Well, we got the PSD 188 car,' said the Inspector. 'Got it at Pilberry.'

'Oh yes, why didn't we think of that?' said Peter. 'We *thought* that fellow lived at Pilberry!'

136

'Bless us all, did you now?' said the Inspector. 'I'm beginning to wonder if there's anything you *don't* know! Well, we got the car, and the dogs. The man has got a shop there, with two or three garages. He'd put the dogs into one of the garages. Goodness knows how many dogs he's stolen and sold. Ah, well PSD stood for Pretty Sick Driver by the time we'd told him all we knew about him!'

'And we also got the old caretaker fellow,' said the sergeant. 'He's a poor old stick, though, a bit feeble-minded, but clever enough to help a dog-stealer, it seems! We wondered where he had gone to earth, and there he was, in this town, under our very noses!'

'We got the young man, too, at Starling's,' said the Inspector. 'He's a bad lot. He and the other man ran this dog-stealing business between them, quite cleverly too. Covered their tracks well all the time, and bamboozled us nicely.

'But they couldn't bamboozle the Secret Seven, could they!' added the Inspector, getting up. 'Well, we must be off. Thanks, all of you. I wish there were more children like you, you're a grand lot to have in our town!'

The two big policemen went out, and the children shut the door and grinned happily at one another.

'Bamboozle,' said Colin, slowly. 'Bamboozle, that would be a fine word for our next password. What about it? Bamboozle, nobody would ever guess that, so long as Jack doesn't write it down for Susie to see!'

'Don't tease him,' said Janet. 'I do feel so happy, what with George back again, and all! What about a round of ice-creams? I've got my Saturday money today. I'll treat you all. Yes, and you too, Scamper darling! If anyone has earned an ice-cream, *you* have!'

'WOOF!' said Scamper, thoroughly agreeing, thumping his tail so hard on the floor that it raised quite a dust. 'WOOF!'

So there go the Secret Seven out into the sunshine, Scamper too. I do really think they're a fine Secret Society, don't you? And I can't help wondering whatever they will be up to next!